Fighting For Life:
Death Riot

Written By **Milan Taplin**

This is a story about 5 kids who face a series of adventures, so enjoy!!
We are all under 11 yrs old. What were you doing at that age? Was your life an ADVENTUREEEEEEEE?!

Table Of Contents

Chapter ONE:

The Beginning

Once upon a time in a city called Hawkville, lived five kids Kylie, Kacion, Jelly, Jayceon and Me, Milan. It was November and our parents were on vacation so we were all alone. HOME ALONE. Like the movie, ya know, home alone or at least we thought....

Me and Kacion were so excited for Halloween we decorated the inside of Jelly's house. We decided to eat popcorn & watch "Home Alone", what a coincidence. When the movie ended Kacion went to go pop some more popcorn because we were going to watch another movie but he didn't. We ran out of butter so we had to

go to the store. The store
was only two blocks away
so we could all walk
together.

As we hurried back
from the corner store an old
man started following us. I
began walking faster as
everyone else caught on &
began to speed up. Then,
Jelly took off running so
we all started to run back to
her house. Next thing you

know, the old man started to run but since he was old he was a slow runner. We had the chance to go home hoping he wouldn't follow us. When we got home with the butter we popped the popcorn and turned on the movie "IT".

(Disclaimer: Okay, so I'm really afraid of the movie "IT" but I'm going to watch it because I'm not going to let them know that. Hahaha. Okay, back to the story!)

But before the movie started we heard a knock on the door. Me, Jayceon & Kacion tip-toed to the door to look through the peephole. It was the old man. Jayceon suddenly pushed all of us out of the way as he stared at the old man, it was his Grandpa. As we let him inside he started telling us why he was following us. He said that he knew who Me, Kacion, Jelly and Jacyeon were but not Kylie and tried to ask who she was and then we started running. Jayceon flopped on the couch & yelled "Woooh, I'm happy that was you because I don't know what we would have done if it was someone else!" as he deeply sighed & grabbed his game controller.

Kacion started laughing "Aww Jayceon u scaredy cat!". He laughed so much his stomach began to hurt. I then screamed "Be quiet Kacion you were scared too, We all were. I know I was, I can't even lie about it." " Be quiet Milan, Leave

my brother alone!" said
Kylie. "Kylie just be quiet,
you were under the sofa
crying, just stop." said
Jayceon as he bent over
holding his stomach in
laughter almost falling off
the sofa. "Aiiight now
that's enough. Relax, I'm
pretty sure everyone was
afraid. It's okay." said
Jayceon's Grandpa.

"Wait a minute, where are y'all parents? Are you here alone? Where's Jelly?" but before we could answer. "BOOM" (something came clashing on the floor). Then, the tv had turned off by itself & Kylie was gone. Everyone looked around at each other & before we could panic Kylie jumped out from behind the couch saying "BOOOOOOOO" she was

trying to scare us, we
weren't scared.

Chapter
TWO:

Just Getting
Started

"Okay , don't forget the question I asked. Are you all here alone?" repeated Jayceon's Grandpa. "No" "Well yeah for now, Jelly mom ran to the market, she'll be back soon!" said Kacion. *I know he lied, but I mean what's a little lie, ya know.* " Good, well I'll sit with you guys for a few minutes, get some rest then I'll be on my way." said Jayceon's Grandpa.

Kylie began grabbing snacks. We grabbed our drinks, candy, ice cream , popcorn & began eating our food. When we finally got the chance to watch the movie the backdoor made a weird noise and we realized Jelly was gone. We searched and searched, she was nowhere to be found. "See I just asked you guys where she was," said Jayceon's Grandpa. We looked in all of the rooms and Kacion found her under her mom's bed. She was hiding from the old man when he knocked on the door. We had to explain who he was.

We were bored so we went to play outside. I noticed a bulletin board for a new fidget spinner. It was only one block away from Jelly's house. Before we walked to the Target where it was sold we had to figure how much money we would spend & how much money we had all together. Kacion said we would waste $30, Jelly said it would only cost $20. There were five of us and the spinners cost six dollars. Kacion asked for my calculator to show Jelly that it would be $30. She got mad. She always gets mad. Jelly was so mad she chased Kacion around the house and tried to hit him with a teddy bear. She started to get tired so she threw the teddy bear at Kacion but the teddy bear hit the TV making it fall on the old man, well Jayceon's Grandpa. He started screaming. Me and Kacion lifted up the tv as Jayceon helped his Grandpa onto the sofa. "Aaaaagh, my back, my back bone hurts!!" exclaimed Jayceon's Grandpa. We all went into the bathroom to discuss what just happened. "Excuse us" said Jelly as we ran into the bathroom. As soon as we got into the bathroom, Jelly burst into laughter. We all began laughing while Kylie started mimicking the old man, well Jayceon's Grandpa.

Chapter <u>THREE</u>:

The Inconspicuous **NOT**

I don't know why I keep saying old man when it's Jayceon Grandpa. I also don't know why I keep saying Jayceon's Grandpa when he has a name. A name unknown, because he never told us his name. Maybe his name is Unknown or Anonymous or maybe it's Maybelline.

All of a sudden lightning struck as we heard a loud scream. "Aaaagh, HELP ME"! We rushed outside just in time to see the old man's body falling down the steps. "NOOOOOO!" yelled Jayceon as he ran down the step to help his Grandpa get up. The rest of us ran inside, scared. Jelly's next door neighbor asked if "Everything was okay" as she heard the old man screaming. Jayceon told her "Everything is fine" as he put his Grandpa's arm around his shoulder and walked side by side with him up the stairs. Meanwhile, inside Jelly was writing Jayceon's Grandpa a letter.

Dear Jayceon's Grandpa,

I hope you are okay. I'm really sad this happened to you. I feel bad for making fun of you now. I hope you feel better, old man.

About 20 minutes later, "WEEE OOOH WEEE, WEEEE OOOH WEEEEE" we hear cop sirens. Someone had called the police.

"Police open up!" yelled an officer. We all scurried around the house then hid in Jelly's closet. Jayceon's Grandpa was on the sofa but he could not move to open the door. "Open up, it's the Police" yelled an officer again. This time we all begin throwing Jelly's blankets on us in the closet to hide. "IIIII can't…" yelled Jayceon's Grandpa as he attempted to lift his

fragile body off of the sofa.
"BANG" was the next
thing we heard as the
Police opened up the front
door & it slammed against
the wall. "Are they dumb?"
"Are they joking?"
"Really?" said several
officers as they walked in
the door. The door was
unlocked. Kacion forgot to
lock the door so all they
had to do was turn the knob
to open it.

Chapter FOUR: The World NEVER Stops

The cops walked in the house and saw the old man on the sofa, moaning in pain. They directed the paramedics to the sofa and let them take the old man out of the house as they searched for **US**…..

The officers searched each crevice of the house and were about to leave when Kacion farted and Kylie yelled " Ill Kacion you stink"! She yelled so loud

I'm pretty sure the whole entire world could hear her. At least that's what it sounded like to me.

All it took was a few seconds and the officers were in the bedroom opening up the closet door moving the blankets off of us, one by one by one.

Chapter FIVE:

Innocent or Guilty

Jail! What is Jail?
How did we get here?
Why are we here?
Wait, what? What is
going on?.......
Thoughts running
through all of our
minds.

When we went to jail
things began to make sense.
Maybe the lady, you

remember the next door
neighbor, right? Maybe she
thought we pushed the old
man down the stairs &
made him hurt himself.
Maybe she called the police
on us. The next day we had
to go to court. In court we
learned the old man's
name, well Jayceon's
Grandpa name, which was
Jefferld Lincoln Stilts.
Pretty weird name. I'm not
sure what is weirder. The

fact that we are in JAIL or his name. I think they are pretty equal. Jefferld Lincoln Stilts, I thought to myself as I chuckled inside. I think the name was weirder but he was still our Grandpa. And we would face every challenge to be FREE again!!

Chapter SIX:

FREEDOM, FREE US!

"**LOSERS**. Why are we here? Didn't they read my letter?", said Jelly.

Losers.

"Ugggggh" exclaimed Jayceon. Face dripping in sweat as he realized he is really in jail. "Can't catch me!" yelled Kacion, jokingly running in place. "You're caught!" said Jelly as she rolled her eyes. She didn't understand how he could play at a time like this. "Heyyyy, let me go!" I said, snatching away from the officer holding my arm in court. "I want to go home!" said Kylie as she flopped on the floor. "Why are we here?" we all said simultaneously.

Chapter SEVEN: Are We DREAMING?

"12 days! 12 days! 12 days! We were in this place for 12 days! This can't be real" I yelled, pulling at my hair. We were all stressed out being in here. I mean we are just kids, we didn't even do anything. "12 days!" Kacion said. Although we don't want to be in here we learned the ropes in jail. We made friends with the guards. Everyday after lunch they gave us special food. They gave us extra blankets and let us all sleep in the same room together. We were too little to be in the adult jail so we had to go to Juvie. Juvie, the Juvenile Detention Center. In four days, we would go to court. It was getting closer and closer to our court day. We were counting

down day by day, hour by
hour, minute by minute.
We were so scared. What
were we going to say ?
Who was going to talk to
the judge? Everyone was
so nervous so all of us
decided to make ME
Milan, our lawyer. You
see age didn't matter since
this case involved a bunch
of nine, seven and five
year olds. I was going to
be our lawyer.

I was **DETERMINED** to get us out of jail. Just then, a commercial came on with the fidget spinner we wanted, it sold out. Now we can't even get our fidget spinner when we get out.

Chapter EIGHT:

Justice

Two days before court but to us it was one day until FREEDOM. By that, I mean one day until Juvie blows up and everybody perishes in a terrible fire. Same thing would happen to the adult jail. ESCAPE! That is what we were going to do.

Our plan was to leave while everybody else was sleeping and the guards weren't paying attention.

Good thing we got in good with the guards because they rarely checked on us making it easy for us not to be detected when we try to escape.

Chapter NINE:

Court or **BLOW**

The day of reckoning has come. **COURT DAY**.
It was **5** o'clock in the morning on court day. We all sat in a circle discussing our plan to escape. Some people thought we should just wait to go to court to get released. Others were mad & wanted revenge. Others were upset, like really upset. **ME**.

We decided after a long conversation to escape. **THAT DAY**. Right there , in that moment. It was really dark outside , I figured this would be the perfect opportunity. Me & Jayceon crept, tiptoeing to the guards desk, looking side to side to make sure no one saw us. As we got to the guard desk, we saw 2 guards. Both asleep.

I quietly walked near them grabbing the door key from the desk. Jayceon stood back, watching to make sure no guards popped up. We quickly walked back to the room & gathered everyone to start our escape.

Chapter TEN: We Are Out!

Getting to be friends with correctional officers has its perks. Hear me out! Over the weeks, we've learned about numerous hidden cameras, lock keys, special chemicals & gadgets and most importantly, THE ROOM. Not just any room, no no no. The Room where we would escape. It is a very small room inside the kitchen that leads to the outside of the building. Kacion and Jayceon found out about this room one evening after playing basketball with the guards & getting ice cream as a snack. Kylie was sleeping, that may have been our only problem trying to escape. She was not heavy though so Kacion just carried her on his back.

Chapter

ELEVEN:

THE
ESCAPE

Kacion carried Kylie on his back while Me & Jelly used one of the guard keys to open up the door where the jail had explosives. We grabbed as much as we could without dropping them. *I know you may be thinking , why would a jail have explosives because I was wondering why they would have explosives.* But Officer Macintosh told us one day that some officers have side jobs where they use explosives and they keep them at the jail. It was pretty weird to me. Unsafe rather. But I'm just a kid, what do I know? Jayceon used the other key to go inside of the safe to grab a bag of "Eli Flower".

Eli Flower:
A poisonous flower
that is toxic from its
root to its tips. The
roots are brown and
they are damaged. It
has an orange top like
a rose. It may look
soothing but it is fatal.

We all looked at eachother and at the same time said " Lets Go". We slowly crept down the hall passing the officers desk, heading to the kitchen. As we got near the kitchen we heard keys rattling. Shhhhhh I signaled to everyone as I put my finger on my lip. Suddenly the rattling stopped.

Chapter Twelve: Caught! **Maybe** or Maybe Not

Hearts pounding.
Deep breaths.
Nervousness.

The key rattling stopped &
we heard a door close. That
was our que. We ran as fast
as we could through the
kitchen straight to THE
ROOM.

Sweaty, fumbling with the keys in my hand, it felt like we were there forever. I just needed to breathe but at the moment I couldn't. Jelly grabbed the keys from me & unlocked the door to THE ROOM as we all ran out. We ran and ran and ran and ran. For miles it felt like. For hours and hours it felt like.

Jelly's house was 10 blocks from where we were. My house was 9 blocks away. Kacion and Kylie's house was 8 blocks away so we decided to go to Jayceon's house which was only 4 blocks away.

Chapter THIRTEEN:

Home, Alone **Again**

We escaped!!!! We all danced in a circle doing our dances. We felt like grown ups. We did a thing. We escaped from jail. Now we had to put together our plan for both Juvie and the adult jail to perish in flames. We counted our dynamite and Eli Flower. It was certain we had more than enough to execute our masterplan.

We waited until 5 in the morning when it was really dark to go outside.

Dressed in all black pants and shirts.
2 black stripes on both sides of our cheeks.
Black gloves and black sneakers.
Bag load of dynamite and Eli Flower.

We all took some dynamite
and Eli flower and placed it
around both jails. They
were next to each other so
it made it easy for us. We
gathered together as Me &
Jayceon went to light the
dynamite beings as though
we are the oldest out of the
bunch. "Runnn, Runnn for
your life" Jelly and Kacion
yelled. As we all took off
running. We ran until we
got to my house. I think we

were so scared that we ran
9 blocks away past
everyone else's house.
Breathing deeply, I said
"I'm going to take a shower
and lay down" as we
rushed through the front
door.

Chapter Fourteen:

Seriously

Milan.

Milannn.

Milannnnnnnn.

"Milan, did you not hear your alarm?" asked my MOM as she walked into my room.

"Mom?" I jumped up asking confusedly, rubbing my eyes.

"Milan, did you not hear me nor your alarm?" asked my Mother again.

"Mom , where am I? When did you get here?" I asked, still confused.

"You are home." said my mom, one eyebrow raised looking at me suspiciously.

"I've been here , what do you mean?" she asked.

"Mom, you were not here." I said , sitting upright in my bed.

"Milan, I've been here. I'm not sure where else I would be. Get up, you have school. It is 6 o'clock in the morning, you need to get ready for school. Did you have a bad dream or something?" questioned my Mom, looking puzzled.

I looked over at my alarm clock and smacked my forehead with my hand as I screeched..

No, No, No, Nooo,
Don't tell me it
was a..
It was a..
Was A..
A…
It was all A
DREAM!!

TO BE CONTINUED.

Made in the USA
Coppell, TX
25 February 2023

13378256R00046